Winslow Anderson

A Description of the Desiccated Human Remains

in the California State mining bureau

Winslow Anderson

A Description of the Desiccated Human Remains
in the California State mining bureau

ISBN/EAN: 9783337369217

Printed in Europe, USA, Canada, Australia, Japan

Cover: Foto ©Andreas Hilbeck / pixelio.de

More available books at **www.hansebooks.com**

CALIFORNIA STATE MINING BUREAU.

WM. IRELAN, JR., STATE MINERALOGIST.

BULLETIN No. 1.

A DESCRIPTION

OF THE

· DESICCATED HUMAN REMAINS

IN THE

CALIFORNIA STATE MINING BUREAU.

By WINSLOW ANDERSON, M.D.

SACRAMENTO:
STATE OFFICE, : : : J. D. YOUNG, SUPT. STATE PRINTING.
1888.

INTRODUCTORY.

*To the honorable Board of Trustees of the California
State Mining Bureau:*

GENTLEMEN: In compliance with your invitation, I
have the honor to submit the. following article on the
mummified human remains now on exhibition in the
Ethnological Department of your Bureau.

Subjoined to the description and measurements of
these ancient bodies I have made a few observations
on: The infancy of the intellectual races and their ethnological classification; some of the habits and foods of
the savages now inhabiting different parts of the globe;
the probable origin of the aborigines of the Pacific
Coast, their historical traditions, burial ceremonies,
myths, etc.—all relating more or less to the existence
of a once flourishing race—the ancestors of our present
mummifications.

In the preparation of the paper I have availed myself of the many interesting and valuable anthropologi-
cal and ethnological data from the pens of some of the
most renowned scientists and writers the world has
ever produced, and it is desired to make due acknowledgment here to all those who have not been mentioned in the body of the article. Prominent among
these are the names of Darwin, Huxley, Spencer,
Haeckel, Cortes, Acosta, Clavigero, Duran, Sahagun,
Diaz, Chaves, Karl, Snell, Hale, Flint, Farrar, Her-
rera, Bancroft, Prescott, De Bourbourg, Powell, and
many daily, weekly, and monthly journals.

Acknowledgment is also due to Mr. W. S. Keyes for his valuable services in taking the photographs of the bodies from which the arto-type plates were secured.

It may be confidently predicted that when the Pacific slope—so rich in prehistoric remains—shall have been thoroughly explored, many interesting and valuable discoveries will be made relative to the origin of the Pacific Coast aborigines and their relationship to the European anthropophagous cave-dwellers.

I have the honor, gentlemen, to subscribe myself your obedient servant,

WINSLOW ANDERSON, M.D.

829 Broadway, San Francisco, May 1, 1888.

NATURALLY MUMMIFIED HUMAN BODIES EXHUMED IN THE SIERRA MADRE MOUNTAINS.

Through the liberality and untiring energy of Mr. J. Z. Davis, President of the Board of Trustees of the State Mining Bureau, a valuable collection of desiccated human remains has been added to the archæological department of this institution.

HISTORY OF THE DISCOVERY.

While the Mexican archæologist, Signor S. Marghieri, was exploring the eastern side of the Sierra Madre Mountains in Mexico, about two hundred miles south of Deming, between Coralitos and Casas Grandes, and at an elevation of nearly seven thousand feet, a hermetically sealed cave was discovered and explored. The floor was nearly smooth, the sides rough and rugged, and the vault covered with stalactites. The cave was of considerable dimensions, and proved to be a veritable sepulchre, for at the far end of this cavern, four mummified human remains were found. The caves which this people sanctified by the inhumation of their dead, are generally situated in the cliffs, on the banks of some large river, or high up some precipitous and almost inaccessible mountain. (See the writer's article in "Science," September 23, 1887.)

The bodies were found in a sitting posture, hands crossed on the breast and knees approaching the chin, with the head inclined forward. They were all carefully shrouded in their burial garments, and accurately placed facing the rising sun—the source of all light—presumably ready to rise at a moment's warning, shake the dust from their heads, and walk out of their sarcophagus. The male and the female (see Figures 1 and 2) probably husband and wife, were seated side by side, the elder child, a boy (Figure 3), was placed to the right of the father, and the younger child, a little girl (Figure 4), to the left of the mother. In addition to the burial shrouds the little girl was enveloped in the skin of an animal, similar to the method used on the islands of Fuerteventura, the better to preserve its tender frame.

Entombed in their cave sepulchre could be found no trace of any implements, utensils, or personal effects. No hieroglyphics or pictographs to indicate their history or give a clew to their identity.

The floor of the cavern, and the remains, were covered with a fine, impalpable dust, probably the accumulation of ages. No footprints of man or beast had desecrated the sepulchre since the time of the interment. Only one sign remained to indicate the advent of man to these now barren and desolate regions (besides the ruins of cities and casas to be noticed elsewhere), and that was the sealing of the opening of the cave. This had been accomplished by means of sun-dried, adobe bricks, and adobe paste, or plaster, together with natural rocks from the mountain. So carefully are these caves sealed that none but an acute observer would notice its artificial closure.

Professor Marghieri and party having determined to convey the bodies to San Francisco, the utmost secrecy was necessary, for it would have been all their lives were worth to have the Indians discover the contents of their parcels. The aborigines of this, and many other localities, entertain the greatest superstitious veneration for their departed ancestors, amounting, in many cases, to actual worship, believing the spirits of the dead, of whom they cherish fabulous accounts, hover over them and their dead bodies, and protect the community from evil. Should the bodies be removed, the spirits would also follow, and the Indians would lose their guardians and spiritual advisers. Indeed, some tribes believe that the spirit resides in the bones of the dead. Hence, whilst the Indians did not know specifically the place of interment of the mummified bodies, their legends teach them that the mountains and caves are peopled with the spirits of some great nation of whom they are pleased to call themselves descendants.

Accordingly, the bodies were carefully wrapped in such cloth as they had, and packed in sacks and strapped on the backs of the pack mules, and conveyed some two hundred miles to the nearest railroad station, where they were carefully repacked in suitable cases, and transported to San Francisco.

Having ascertained their whereabouts, Mr. J. Z. Davis lost no time in purchasing the bodies, and generously presented them to the State Mining Bureau, where they form one of the many notable attractions that are daily viewed by hundreds.

Aside from their great curiosity, as being among the first natural mummifications discovered on this coast, these well preserved human remains present a great many points of general and scientific interest.

DESCRIPTION OF THE BODIES.

These naturally mummified bodies differ from mummies proper, in the general acceptation of the term, inasmuch as no embalming process for their preservation was used. They were desiccated in their cave sepulchre by the natural elements. The dry hot atmosphere extracted all the moisture from the tissues, and the bodies literally dried up as we would dry jerk-beef, or as the Indians of to-day dry the bison (buffalo) meat which keeps for years.

There is no evidence of these bodies having undergone any preparatory process. The brain, heart, lungs, abdominal, and pelvic viscera are all intact and dried to a solid consistency.

Figure 1 (*a and b*) represents the powerful frame of a male body, about five feet eight inches tall and well proportioned. The bones are large, and he must have had an excellent physique. He probably weighed between one hundred and eighty and two hundred pounds. All the body now weighs is fourteen pounds!

The integument is well preserved, and presents the appearance of dried hide, or thick parchment, of a dark gray color, and all that remains between it and the bones are the dried muscles, tendons, nerves, and fascia. The body is well developed, the shoulders measuring from one acromion process to the other, three hundred and ninety millimetres (about fifteen and a half inches); the hands are small, and the fingers tapering; the feet are also small, measuring two hundred and forty millimetres (about nine and a half inches), and highly arched. The phalanges of the digits are perfect, each having the

Fig. 1 a.

Fig. 1 B.

normal number of bones, and the ungual appendages
are well preserved and not unusually long.

The body has dried in the sitting posture, hands
crossed and knees drawn towards the chin. It will be
observed that the cheek and lips on the left side protrude. This probably occurred during the time of
mummification; the moisture leaking from the interior
of the brain and surrounding tissues, through the cribriform plate of the ethmoid at the anterior portion of the
calvaria, through the cribriform foramina into the inferior
meatus nasi, and the head being inclined toward the
left, produced this bulging from the force of gravitation.
Being itself in turn dried up, the mouth maintained its
present shape. Short stiff hairs can be seen on the
head. The eyebrows and eyelashes are also distinctly
visible. A little hair can also be noticed on the upper
lip, but very little beard anywhere on the face. The
ears are closely pressed against the sides of the head
and only the cartilages remain. The eyes are quite
perfect, and present a slight outward obliquity. The
nose, originally broad, has been more flattened by the
shrinking of the cartilages and the alae nasi. The lips
are stiff and solid and the tongue is shriveled to the
consistency of cork. There is a full set of masticators
in his mouth, thirty-two in number, and all quite well
preserved. A few of the dentures only have the enamel
worn down to the dentine. The ribs are large and well
formed, indicative of a well shaped chest. The genita-
lia are well preserved.

It will be observed that on the head there has been
a large growth of hair, on the face very little, and on
the body scarcely any at all.

CRANIAL MEASUREMENTS.

(Figures 1, *a and b.*)

Owing to the dried integument and facia covering the cranium, accurate measurements of the skull are well nigh impossible. The following measurements, however, have been made with as much care and accuracy as the subject permitted. The cranial measurements are as follows:

Circumference, 530 millimetres; length occipito frontal, 178 mm.; breadth bi-bregmatic, 140 mm.; breadth of frontal, 108 mm.; height, 135 mm.; facial angle, 71°.

The sutures and wormian bones can not be inspected. The maler bones are quite prominent and the lower maxillary and face may be classified with the group, orthognathous.

A careful study of this mesocephalic head would indicate that its possessor was of more than average intelligence. The perceptives are well developed. And, although the animal passions undoubtedly predominate, there is enough veneration or religion to class it among the scaphocephalic skulls.

Figure 2 *(a and b)* represents all that is earthly of what was once a woman and a mother. She is in a better state of preservation than the preceding body. From a measurement of the individual bones, she would be about five feet five inches tall, and weighed, perhaps, about one hundred and fifty to one hundred and seventy pounds. The body weighs, in its present condition, only twelve pounds! The posture, integument, body,

Fig. 2 a.

Fig. 2 B.

etc., resemble the one previously described. A rare chance is here given for the examination of the internal organs (see Figure 2, *b*), owing to an absence of integument on the major portion of the right side. The lungs resemble a dried sponge in appearance, and the heart looks like a dried piece of meat. The great blood vessels, and the abdominal and pelvic viscera can be explored, and with the exception of being all shriveled up, there is no anomaly, either in position or arrangement. The large, oval pelvis, and the once well developed mammæ bear unmistakable evidence of gestation. The hands and feet are small and well shaped; the foot measuring only two hundred and fifteen millimetres (about eight and one half inches). On the head will be seen a luxuriant growth of hair, which centuries have not yet succeeded in destroying. It is very fine in texture, of a dark brown color, and entirely unlike any Indian hair seen to-day. A curious feature is observed in connection with the small, well proportioned ears, both of which are perfectly preserved, and that is, in each lobe is worn, even in the stillness of death, a piece of hollow bamboo or reed, about forty millimetres in length, and ten millimetres in diameter. This was likely considered an ornament in her day. Our Indians of to-day pierce the helix and anti-helix of the ear, through which holes they suspend ornaments of different kinds. The single perforation in the lobe of this mummified woman's ear would indicate a custom observed by her people, similar to the customs in vogue in the more civilized countries, and are not usually observed by Indians of our own period.

The windows of the soul, although now sightless and

dim, are singularly perfect, presenting a slightly outward and upward obliquity of the external canthi.

The nose is also quite perfect, and inclined to be rather broad and flat than thin and protruding. The maler bones are very prominent. The lips thin and stiff, and the tongue dried and solid. Two central incisores and one canine of the superior maxillary are gone, and several other teeth are badly caried.

CRANIAL MEASUREMENTS.

(Figures 2, *a and b.*)

Here, again, the same difficulty of hair and dried integument prevent absolutely accurate measurements. The skull measures: Circumference, 503 millimetres; length, occipito frontal, 166 mm.; breadth, bi-bregmatic, 128 mm.; breadth of frontal, 103 mm.; height, 132 mm.; facial angle, 69°.

This skull presents a large forehead and well developed reasoning powers. The woman was likely filled with noble instincts and motherly kindness. It is very rare to find so good a head among Indian women of to-day.

Figure 3 is the mummified remains of a little boy about seven years old. The little fellow had been enveloped in his burial shrouds the same as the larger bodies—hands crossed on the chest, knees doubled on the breast, and the head inclined forward. All the bodies were likely tied in this position when placed in the cave. The body is about three feet tall, and weighs now only three pounds! The same general characteristics as to skin, tissues, bones, etc., that were observed

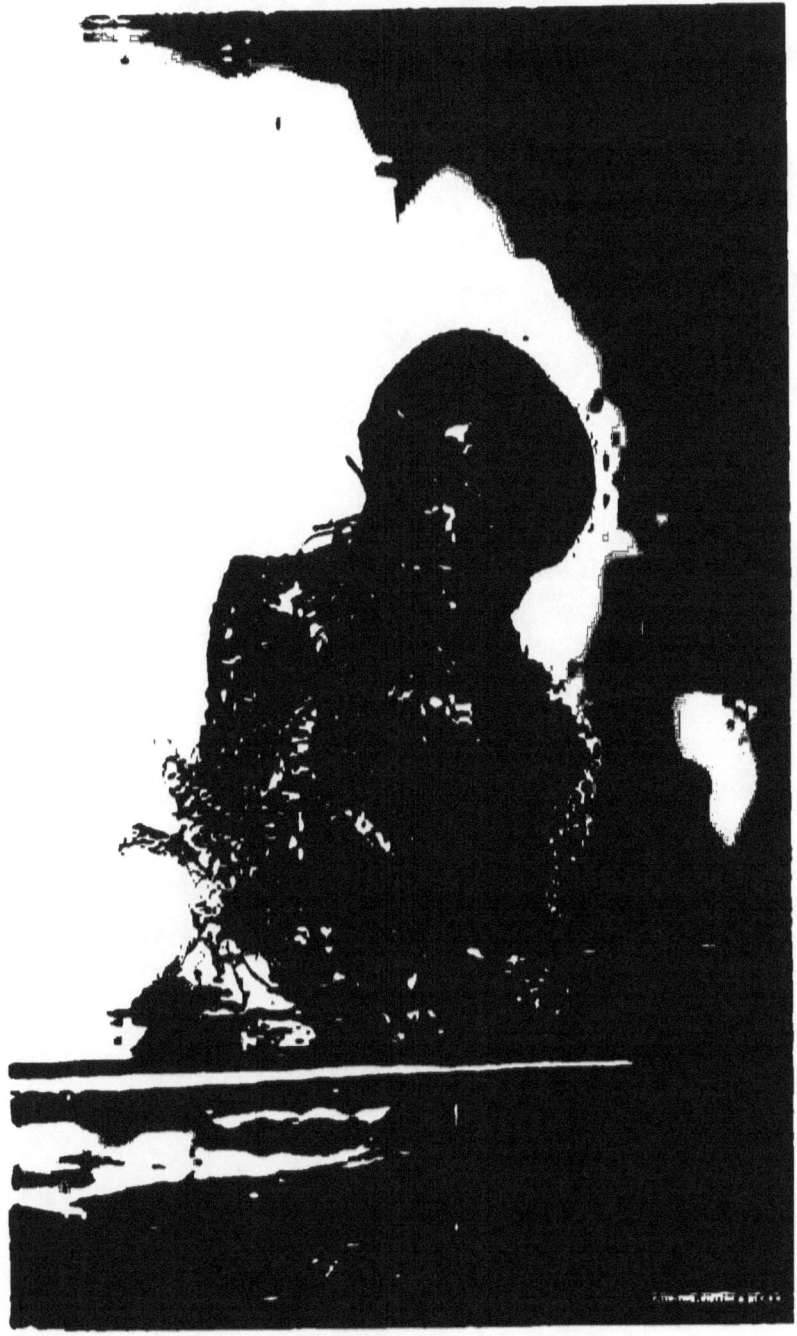

Fig. 3.

Fig. 4.

in the preceding bodies, may also be seen here. The head is well developed for a boy of his age. The hair has been broken off near the scalp. Only the cartilagenous parts of the ears remain. There is the same contour of face—flat nose, high cheek bones, outward obliquity of the eyes, etc. The upper and lower incisores and canine of the temporary or milk teeth are gone, and the permanent set coming at their roots in the alveolar processes.

The two anterior molars of the superior maxillary are just appearing through the alveolar processes, establishing the age with tolerable accuracy at about seven years.

CRANIAL MEASUREMENTS.

In circumference the skull measures 440 millimeters; length, occipito frontal, 146 mm.; breadth, bi-bregmatic, 120 mm.; breadth of frontal, 60 mm.; height, 114 mm.; facial angle, 71°.

Considerable of his burial shrouds remains about the body yet. The major portion of it is cotton fabric, firmly secured around the body by a stronger cord, made of braided hair.

Figure 4 is all that is earthly of a little girl, about fourteen to eighteen months of age. She weighs only a pound and a half!

The little one has been enveloped in an animal's skin, the better to protect its tender frame. Both feet are gone, and the tibiæ and fibulæ protrude through the skin. The four upper and four lower incisores, with the corresponding canine teeth, have made their appearance, showing the child to be about fourteen to eighteen months old.   Otherwise the same features are noticeable in this as in the preceding figures.   .

It would appear that the group of four belong to one family, and that they were buried by friends, and hermetically sealed in this cave for fear of some real or imaginary foe.   It may have been at the time of the Spanish invasion, or it may have been during the warlike times anterior to this date, when the Aztec confederation was warring with the Toltec people.

From their physical and mental developments the race seems to have been a superior one.

The facial features observed in these bodies are not those we find in that locality now.   The cranial configurations and physical appearances would rather favor Aztec lineaments than those of our Indian of to-day. The fine dark brown hair is certainly not Indian, nor do the small hands and feet bear much resemblance to the huge hands and feet we see on the Indians now living.   It is not desired to be understood that a race or classification can be even approximately established by the measurements of a few crania; for it can not.   It only aids us in determining that particular individual's peculiarities.   Too many ethnological classifications have been advanced on the measurements of a few skulls and on the descriptions of a few bodies.   Measure, for example, a few skulls of any race, and see how much they differ in the very essentials of capacity, circumference, length, breadth, height, facial angle, etc., that go far in the classification of ethnologists.   We may draw attention to the similarity existing between these bodies and the Asiatics, for instance, but we cannot *a priori* establish a relationship, nor can we positively determine from our present data that these bodies are Toltecs or Aztecs, however much our own views may favor such a theory.

BURIAL SHROUDS.

The fabrics found on the bodies, forming the burial shrouds, are chiefly composed of cotton, hair, hide, grasses, and the bark of willows. The cotton is twisted and coarsely woven, each thread being from a half to one millimetre in diameter. The hair is treated in like manner occasionally, although usually it is braided with three or four divisions in each cord. Frequently we find strong strands made of strips of hide covered with willow bark.

Although the weaving of this interesting people is that known as the "plain" process, that is, where the weft passes alternately under and over the threads of the warp, producing more or less open mesh cloth, yet considerable skill and ingenuity were observed in the manufacturing of their blankets, mats, and ornamental cloths, which were frequently interwoven with beads and colored threads, presenting various designs. Grasses and straws were also woven into mats and cloths, which were of great durability. The skins of animals were also used for clothing purposes.

OBSERVATIONS ON THE INFANCY OF THE INTELLECTUAL RACES.

The origin of the human family has ever been shrouded in the deepest of mysteries. Scholars of the first eminence have given to the world the results of their researches, but, unfortunately, no two of them are agreed. We may accept any one of the three prominent hypotheses, each one of which has been so ably advocated, from the days of Camper and Blumenbach, down to our own time.

The first, or special creation theory, is that of the monogenists. It teaches that Adam and Eve were created in the alluvial valleys of Asia, and brings to its aid the records of holy writ. Many of the most renowned ethnologists and thinkers of the age support this hypothesis. Anatomically considered, there is no difference between a Caucasian and an Ethiopian, or a Caucasian and an Indian, except, perhaps, the contour of the skull and face, stature, etc. Bone for bone, however, they are anatomically alike. It is observed that climate, habits, etc., account largely for the difference in the color of the skin, texture of the hair, etc., and true it is, a vine grown in the dark is found to be translucent, and almost colorless. Likewise the bear is white in the Arctic region, brown in the temperate, and black at the equator, although anatomically allied.

Man, unlike animals, the monogenists claim, is a direct issue of the creative, or divine power, and that the Hebraic record is the only solution of the origin of things.

The polygenistic, or second theory of the creation of man, teaches us that there was not only *one*, but that there were *several* special creations—one for each race, and that climatic surroundings do not account for all the diversities and differences found in the human race. The learned ethnological authorities advocating the polygenistic theory, argue that the Mosaic account is true, but that it only includes the history of one race. These authorities, although directly antagonistic in many of their views, must be received with due respect, owing to the distinguished positions they have earned in the many branches of anthropology.

During the last fifty or hundred years these two prominent theories have not materially changed.

The third hypothesis, that of evolution, is of more recent birth, and although it may be more repugnant to the *quasi* scientific mind, it is nevertheless truly scientific. We are all more or less familiar with the evolution of life as witnessed in the infusorial animalcula in water, spores in the air, generation of fungi in cereals, and birth, as it were, rising out of death. In a few hours a decayed cabbage head, or a putrescent piece of meat, under favorable conditions of temperature and moisture, will teem with new life. It is not desired to be understood that an extreme view of evolution is advocated, or even implied, for it is not believed possible to evolve, generate, or create organic life in the laboratory out of inorganic elements. The egg whose germinal vesicle has not been fertilized by the male bird cannot bring forth a chick, nor can inorganic atoms bring forth organic life.

Through countless ages, natural selection, the survival of the fittest, continual advancement, development, and improvement have at last evolved man in his present condition. The human species has reached its ultimatum of physical perfection. The *fixity* of *type* is stamped on the human embryo long before it is discoverable by man. Naturalists point out the anatomical similarity between man and beast. In his embryonic

2

state man cannot be differentiated from the wolf or the horse by the most powerful microscope or by the most delicate analysis. The germs of the embryos of the tortoise at the fourth week, the chick at the fourth day, the dog at the fourth week, and man at the fourth week, are alike insusceptible of differential demonstration. Physiologically and chemically they are identical. Indeed bold thinkers of the present day assert that man is not a biped, and that his natural mode of locomotion is on four instead of on two limbs. The *foramen magnum* would certainly indicate that the head was originally in a horizontal relation to the vertebræ, and the sacrum and coccyx bear a strong resemblance to the caudal extremity in animals.

ETHNOLOGICAL CLASSIFICATIONS.

On the next stepping-stone—ethnology, or the science which treats of the classification or races of man—we find monogenists, polygenists, and evolutionists, again trying to unite their forces in analyzing and classifying humanity.

Thus we find that Virey gives only two races of men on the globe. Cuvier makes three. Linnæus increases them to four. The great Blumenbach issues five, Buffon six, Peschel seven, and the renowned Agassiz eight different races. Pickering comes with eleven, and the learned Fredrich Müller assures us that there are twelve. Bory de St. Vincent sees fifteen. America's greatest anthropologist, Morton, increases the number to twenty-two, while Crawford has sixty and Burke sixty-three special creations. These classifiers represent the highest authority of which the world can boast, men who have devoted their lives and powerful intellects to the intricate problem. Doubtless they would all agree had they adopted the same standard of comparison, but one distinguishes a race by geographical location; another by language, habits, and mental traits; another by stature, contour of skull and face; another proposes the color of the skin, and still another the texture of the hair; while the most acute observers combine all the distinctions and characteristics, and still they give us from *two* to *sixty different* human races.   *Walter W. B*

Adopting whatever classification you may, and accepting whichever theory of creation you will, we can almost admit that there is not as much difference between the higher forms of apes and the lower forms of savages as there is known to exist between the highest and the lowest forms of humanity, when we look at the races existing to-day on nearly all parts of the globe. If the poor miserable savages are not actually below the brute creation, they are certainly not very far above it. Look at the Fuegian, for instance, crawling from the lair in which he lies, coiled up like an animal on the wet ground, to gather the food on which he subsists, mussels and berries, whenever hunger demands it. On state occasions they vary their bill of fare by killing and eating their old women. Their language is an inarticulate clacking. The negroes of New Guinea live on the trees, and spring from branch to branch, like monkeys, gesticulating, screaming, and laughing, and eke out their living on the indigenous fruits, as do the apes themselves. The Alforese of Ceram also live in trees, like the birds, each family being in perpetual hostility with every other family, human and animal.

The forest tribes of Malacca communicate by means of noises very similar to the native birds. Again, the Dyaks hunt and kill the wild people of Borneo as if they were monkeys. The cannibal Fans of equatorial Africa bury their corpses for several days before they eat them.

In Chinese cities rats are sold at fifty cents per dozen for the table. The hind quarters of the dog command a higher price than those of lamb or mutton. In Brazil ants are eaten alive with resinous and spicy sauces. In Africa they are stewed in grease. The East Indians catch the ant in pits and wash them in handfuls, and eat them. One of the most costly dishes in Siam is a curry made of ants' eggs. Shrimps are eaten alive by the Sandwich Islanders. The Singalese eat the bees after robbing them of their honey.

The negroes of the West Indies eat baked snakes and worms fried in fat. In the Pacific Islands lizards and their eggs are considered wholesome. Roasted spiders are used for dessert by the New Caledonians.

A pigmy race in South Abyssinia, the Dokos, grow their nails like the talons of the vulture to enable them to dig up ants and tear in pieces the flesh of serpents, both delicacies which they eat raw. Most any animal compares favorably with the fierce Bosjesman, whose diet is composed of worms, beetles, and pismires, unless he can share with the hyena the putrid carcass of a buffalo or an antelope. A gibberish speech, like the growling of a mad dog, is the language of the Yamparico, who lives on roots, crickets, and different species of bugs. The aborigines of Victoria live on roots, grubs, mushrooms, and frogs, with an occasional feast in the shape of a new born baby, killed, roasted, and eaten by the parents and friends. The locust plague on the Pacific Coast in 1875, sent by the Great Spirit, was a source of worshipful thanksgiving to the Digger Indians, who dug large pits, swarmed them full of locusts, which they killed, dried, and ground to powder in their stone mortars, and thus laid in a store of food which lasted them for several years.

The Russians use the fermented liquid of cabbage for their beverage. It is called "quass," and may be described as resembling in taste a mixture of stale fish, washed in soapsuds; and next to beer, more civilized (?) people drink it, than any other beverage.

After they have wound the silk from the cocoon, the Chinese eat the chrysalis of the silkworm. In Mexico, parrots are eaten, and in the Argentine Republic, skunks are much sought after for the table. The African bushmen are very fond of spiders, and caterpillars are very dainty and costly.

The most ghastly ornamentation I have known is worn by the houseless, mischievous, and vindictive Andamer; it consists of a row of skulls, worn around the naked necks of this form of humanity. The Bannaks wear lumps of fat meat, artistically suspended from the cartilages of the nose.

It seems, indeed, hard for us to look back upon our ancestors, as a miserable anthropophagous population, maintaining an inglorious struggle with the powers of nature, wrestling with naked bodies against the forest animals, and frequently forced to dispute their cave dwellings with the hyena and the wolf, and yet we have but to look at the leather-skinned Hottentot, whose hair grows in short tufts, with bare scalp between, and is only a creature of passions, feelings, and appetites.

Look at the wild people of Borneo, the Negrilloes, of Armanga; the Battas, of Sumatra; the hairy Ainos, of Jesso; the Hyglous, of the White Nile; the Aborigines, of India; and even the Cagots, and other mandities of France and Spain. These species, and we must call them human, with squalid habits, ugly and deformed heads, hideous aspect, and prognathous faces, have probably lived as long, and perhaps longer, than the Caucasians; and, as Darwin observes, they are supposed to enjoy a sufficient share of happiness and comfort (of whatever kind it may be) to render life worth having.

Many races on different parts of the globe attribute their origin, not to the gods or demigods, not even to lions, as do the Sahos, or to goats, as do the Dagalis, not to the sun or moon, as do many of the Pacific Coast tribes, but to *apes*. This has been the cherished belief for ages among the Miantsee or aborigines of China, a country whose boasts of creation antedates ours by many thousands of years. The Thibetans and many African tribes also lay claim to the ape as a forefather.

Whilst not advocating evolution *per se*, we are almost forced to admit its possibility on purely scientific grounds, even to the extent of evolving man through the countless ages of the earth's existence, out of—not inorganic atoms or molecules, but out of flesh and blood, by the aid of the All-wise Creative power. As Professor Le Conte says: "I believe that the spirit of man was developed out of the *anima* or conscious spirit of animals, and that this, again, was developed out of lowest forms of life-force, and this in turn out of the chemical and physical forces of nature; and that at certain stages in this gradual development, viz., with man, it acquired the property of immortality precisely as it now, in the individual history of each man at a certain stage, acquires the capacity of abstract thought."

The following striking example shows what can be done in *one* generation in the way of transforming a land animal into one capable of living entirely in water. By taking the embryo of the land salamander out of its egg and keeping it in water at a moderate temperature, abundantly supplied with oxygen, and amply fed with small living water animals, its organism will change. The embryo inhales the oxygen held between the molecules of water, and not the atmosphere, like its parents, breathing with lungs. The embryonic lungs therefore remain undeveloped, but, by way of compensation, small gills will appear on each side of its head. This function of breathing by the gills will gradually increase as the body grows. Feeling the necessity to swim and not to creep as do its land parents, the four extremities become mere rudimentary appendages, while, on the other hand, a vigorous rudder tail develops. The new function of swimming calls forth fins, and the animal actually develops new organs which the parents did not possess. This is a simple experiment which can be accomplished by any one with a little trouble. Thus we find substantially a new animal is produced which elsewhere does not exist. This proves that new organs and new functions are developed when necessary to the individual's existence; in other words, evolution, pure and simple.

There is nothing incompatible or inconsistent in such a view with the Mosaic records; and I am proud to say that the days of theological narrow-mindedness and denunciation of scientific truths are happily disappearing, and seeking as true an investigating channel as does the snow on the mountain side under the influence of the sun's rays seek the proper channel for its sparkling waters.

The three great Bishops of the Church of England (1887) are the pioneers in this noble line of inquiry—development (evolution). An extract from one will suffice: "* * * And to what are we indebted for that potent word, which, as the wand of a magician, has at the same moment so completely transformed our knowledge, and dispelled our difficulties? To modern science, resolutely pursuing its search for truth, in spite of popular obloquy, and—alas! that one should have to say it—in spite, too, often of theological denunciation." [*Bishop of Manchester.*

SOME OBSERVATIONS ON THE ORIGIN OF THE ABORIGINES OF THE PACIFIC COAST.

The origin of our Western Indians, like that of all the other American aborigines, is shrouded in as much darkness and as many uncertainties as the origin of the human family itself. Nearly every nation, and almost every country, has claimed for itself ancestral relationship to our American Indian. Authorities advance the opinion that the red man is a descendant of the ten lost tribes of Israel. Others, that the Indians are Phœnician merchants. Scandinavia, Iceland, and Greenland lay very strong claim to them. Japanese junks are said to have wafted across the ocean and struck on these western shores and peopled America. Carthaginians are said to have shipwrecked on the eastern coast. The Polynesian Islands, Australia, Africa, and Asia alike receive their quota; but before we accept any of the traditions, or even the most popular of these, viz.: that one or two races, springing from the banks of the river Oxus, in the alluvial valleys of Asia, wandered here and there by land and by sea, and thus peopled the whole world, let us listen to the aborigines of America themselves, who furnish us with many interesting and remarkable accounts of their own origin, which, in some respects, simulate that of the civilized races. Take, for example, the Maya or Quiché empire, which was in a high state of civilization at the time of the Christian era. Extensive and complicated political and religious observances were in vogue, massive temples were reared, and the priests and kings had full sway.

The Quiché nation is, perhaps, richest in mythology. Their version of creation is as follows:

The Great Spirit, having, by one word, created this globe out of the clouds, having created all the flora and fauna, and made this earth like heaven itself, and, being justly proud of His work, He commanded the creatures to send forth praise and thanksgiving for their existence. But, no; the dumb brutes failed to obey the mandate. The Great Spirit, becoming angry at such ingratitude, cursed the animals, relegating them to have their flesh torn from their bones, and be killed and eaten. (Hence the origin of eating animal flesh.)   Having satisfied his wrath, the cloud God called a council, and it was arranged to make man, that he might sing praises to his Creator. Accordingly, man was made of clay, and much was expected of him.   When, however, it was time for praise service, the clay man was found to be without volition or speech.   This greatly enraged the cloud gods, and the poor clay man was ordered to be instantly killed. He was, accordingly, drowned forthwith.

After long and careful deliberation, another man was made. This time of wood, as the clay was considered too heavy. A woman was also made to keep him company. Although the man was wooden, his companion was made of pitch—a good combination. Every thing went well for awhile, and the moon, who now took a hand in creation, peopled the whole world with wooden manikins. Intelligence seems to have been at a low ebb, for our wooden kingdom soon forgot to sing praises to the clouds, whereupon the Heart of Heaven became very much angered, and rained *thick, hot resin night and day* on the poor wooden men and women, and killed them all, excepting a very few penitent ones. These surviving few may be seen to this day, living in the forest in happiness, never forgetting to sing praises to their cloud Gods. These wooden people are known to this day as apes or monkeys. After these several trials the Great Spirit was discouraged, and creation was given up for awhile. Nevertheless, at length His wrath subsided, and the other gods prevailed upon Him to try once more his creative power. This time man was to be made as nearly perfect as the gods themselves. The Great Master accordingly made four men and four women out of yellow and white maize, which grew abundantly on the earth in the meantime. These new corn people gave general satisfaction, and their Creator has permitted them to people the world.

The Aztecs were created in an entirely different manner. Their account of creation is in this wise: The God and Goddess in the sky were blessed with a male offspring in the shape of a flint knife. Having several other children in their heavenly abode, it was feared that this hard-hearted flint son would do mischief, and to secure the serenity of heaven His Flint Majesty was cast out of the clouds forever. In his aerial flight, the Flint Son of God fell into the seven caves on this earth and dashed into six thousand and six hundred pieces. Immediately there sprang up six thousand and six hundred demigods from the pieces of the Flint Son. That they might have servants and companions as became their rank, the mother Goddess was implored. She directed them to make application

to Hades for a bone and when obtained to sprinkle it
with their own blood.   One of the most valiant was
forthwith sent to the Infernal region to crave a bone
from his Satanic Highness.   It appears that this
domain was already well supplied with bones, and tra-
dition has it that prior to this present creation the earth
was peopled with giants, but the cloud Gods sent them
all to the lower regions, hence the supply of bones
there.   The bone was obtained by the messenger, but
owing to some slight misunderstanding with the keeper
of Hades a hasty retreat was deemed expedient, and a
fall caused the bone to break, so that when earth was
again reached only a handful of bone was left.   The
few pieces, however, were carefully sprinkled with
blood and in a few days a pretty little maiden sprang
up from each little splinter.   Thus do the Aztecs boast
of their genealogy from both God and the Devil.

According to the Tezcucan annals the sun sent a
dart—one of its beams—through the earth in Mexico,
thereby producing a large hole, out of which man
sprung, full grown.

The Hyperboreans attribute their origin to our common canine.   The Neeshenam were created by the
moon.

Plants and animals are worshiped as creators.   Old
Sol comes in for his share of the praise of creation
among several of the aborigines.

The tribes of Lower California believe that their
souls retreat to some of the verdant isles of the sea,
there to await the birth of some infant, whose body is
occupied by the departed spirit.

Many of these creative myths resemble those of the

old world, especially the Asiatic, which may point to Asia, as Mr. Powers remarks, as the probable origin of some of our aborigines.

From the language, our American aborigines may be of common origin, either indigenous or foreign, or they may be from widely different sources and races, as we have on the Pacific Coast alone over six hundred different tongues.

Language has latterly gained much ground as a crucial test in the determination of the origin of races. Taken conjointly with craniology, facial angles, stature, color of skin, microscopical structure of the hair, and geographical distribution, it certainly must add materially to these data. Taken singly, care must be exercised, or the errors will be as glaring as those frequently committed by craniologists when they pronounce crania as belonging to this or that race, by merely examining half a dozen skulls.

Probably the most reasonable view to take of the origin of the aborigines is this: That different parts of the Western Hemisphere were peopled by different races or nations, or if we accept the polygenistic theory of creation, why the Indian was created contemporaneously with Adam and Eve. Evolution can help us out still more, for the same process that was going on in the old world may also have gone on in the new, the geological advantages remaining on American soil.

People the new world as you please, subdivide the aborigines according to any ethnological data you will, and I believe it will appear quite within speculative bounds to consider Anáhuacs or Toltecs and Aztecs of Asiatic origin.

Their fragmentary history, and pictorial writings would indicate that they came from the far northwest. If the Toltec and Mayo-Quiché empires flourished and rivaled in splendor and culture, in the magnificence of their temples and palaces, and in their complicated systems of religion and politics, those of the old world at the beginning of the Christian era, as it is claimed they did, then all must admit that it would have taken thousands of years to perfect or evolve such systematic governments.

Several similar characteristics can be traced to the Aztecs and the Asiatics, and indeed the Malays and Egyptians. Similar cranial contours and measurements. The hair on the head and the universal absence of beards and the scanty supply of hair on other parts of the body. Small hands and feet. The basic axis of the skull is short, flattened occiput and scaphocephalous crania. Prominent cheek bones. Outward and upward obliquity of eyes. The nose is rather broad than prominent,—color of the skin, and stature generally.

It is certainly within speculative bounds to consider the Eskimos or Innuits, Chukchees (Tsau-chu) and Chukluk-Mut inhabiting Eastern Siberia; the Okee-og-Mut, inhabiting the islands of Behrings Straits; the Aleuts-Aziag-Muts, etc., Kaviag-Mut; the Tinneh-Koyu-Kukhotana, Tenan-Kut-Chien, etc., and the Tlinkets-Chilk-aht-Kwan, Sitka-Kwan, etc., inhabiting American soil, of common stock, modified in the course of centuries by their pursuits, mode of living, environments, etc.

It would, also, be quite natural for these people to

migrate southward to a warmer climate and more pro-
ductive soil, and thus extend along the coast to Mexico
and Central America. This southward migration of
northern tribes does take place. The scientific world
is pretty well agreed that man has inhabited this globe
at least one hundred thousand years in his present form.
As many geological and morphological, as well as topo-
graphical changes have occurred within the known
period of four thousand years, may it not also be possible that America and Asia were united by land at
some time during this vast period?

It has been suggested to my mind that the Pacific
Islands, Hawaii, Friendly, etc., bear evidence of this
union at a period when the American continent was
but a few islands in a vast ocean. In that event inter-
communication was not impossible, nor would it be
were the Pacific twice as broad as it is now.

We can also trace some similarity between certain
religious rites. I will mention but one or two. Many
of the American aborigines bury their dead and supply
the graves with food and drink for months and years.
The wily Chinese spread a sumptuous repast when a
notable dies and place large sums of money near the
dead to pay his way with in the next world; of recent
date, however, the living eat the food and spiritualize
the money in the shape of counterfeit to swindle the
devil. This can be seen at any time at a Chinese
funeral. The counterfeit money is thrown along the
road that the devil may stop to pick it up and so allow
the Celestial to be buried in peace.

HISTORICAL SKETCH OF THE PACIFIC COAST ABORIGINES.

In the sixth century we find the Anáhuac nation enjoying a high state of civilization. Their traditions and pictorals tell us they came from the far north. The pictorals, yet extant, are printed on long strips of cotton and prepared skins with bright red paint. They also carved on wood and stone. They built palaces, temples, and large cities.

In the eleventh century the Chichimecs and Aztecs, also coming from the far north, drove out the Toltecs (who went farther south) and occupied the vanquished country. The Aztecs from "Aztlan," the name of their ancient abode, or "Iztac," meaning white, soon gained supremacy, and although the Toltecs occupied a larger extent of country and attained a far higher degree of civilization, the Aztecs left us the best American language and the most complete history.

Large pyramids were erected at Cholula and Teotihuacan, probably near the Christian era, certainly prior to the sixth century.

Tenochtitlan, or Mexico, was founded early in the fourteenth century by the Aztecs. Traditionally, all the Aztec confederation, or Mexican races, came from the far northwest, and it is computed by the best authorities we have, that prior to the Christian era, as high a state of civilization existed in Mexico and Central America as could be found on any other part of the globe.

At the Spanish invasion the Aztecs occupied large

cities, with magnificent temples and palaces, parks and gardens, and enjoyed a superior system of politics, and advanced religious views for the age.

The splendor of Montezuma's empire rivaled the orientals. His palaces were decorated with solid gold and silver, and inlaid with precious stones. His family and household numbered several thousands, among whom may be mentioned one thousand wives, and almost as large a number of concubines. The customs and ceremonies of this powerful people are very unique and interesting, but want of space precludes more than a brief outline of some of their ceremonies attending the death and funeral rites.

When an Aztec of note was taken ill, the medicine man, relatives, and family were sent for, and solemn council was held. The simpler remedies of indigenous herbs, etc., were given. If these failed and a fatal issue was threatening, perhaps the "sweat house" would be prescribed. If the patient was not cured and still survived the treatment, the medicine man would sit for hours and bark like a dog at the poor patient.

If this failed, dust or water was thrown on the face, and lastly, incantations were used to drive out the devil. Generally, however, the patient died during the process of the treatment.

In the meantime active preparations were making for the funeral. The ceremony varied according to the mode of burial.

If cremation be practiced the body would lie in state for several days. The relatives and slaves of the household would neither eat nor drink for two days, at the end of which time, the general funeral feast was pre-

8

paring, and eating and drinking *ad libitum* was indulged in. Then all follow the remains to the funeral pyre in the temple. Many of the slaves and several of the relatives and frequently the favorite wives were slain, to go with their lord and master, that he may not want for comfort and may not be alone in the spirit land. It was considered an honor to die with a noble, for then, it was believed, that all would go to the highest heaven together.

The funeral pile is burning, music is playing to keep away evil spirits, the people moan and cry, and the victims shriek and struggle as they are forcibly led up to the altar, and thrown on their backs by four strong priests. A knife is now plunged into the poor victim's breast, and the heart is torn out, yet bleeding, and beating with the life that is scarcely extinct!

Immediately the heart is thrown on the funeral pyre of the deceased noble, and the victim's body is either consumed on a separate pile or taken home and eaten by the surviving relatives and friends. This sacred rite continues until the dead noble has enough wives and slaves with him to attend to his comforts in heaven (?). Several dozen people have been known to follow their chief to the next world in the manner above described. On other occasions the dead are buried in caves, and also in graves with their wives and effects.

The following remarkable burial custom obtains with the Mosquitos: The dead body is wrapped in fine cloth, and placed in a wooden coffin in his own house. Music is played to lull him to peaceful rest. In the meantime women inflict on themselves all kinds of torture, tear their hair out, cut their arms and faces, beat their heads against the ground, and cry and shriek until they are exhausted. The men dance and yell, and drink "pulque" or "teuvetli" until they are drunk. This continues for several days. All at once four naked men, with their bodies painted so that the devil cannot recognize them, rush into the dead man's house, seize the coffin, and drag it to the place of interment. The music and mourners follow. The body is placed in the cave or grave, and a tent is erected over it, which is daily provided with food and drink for one year. Should the birds eat the food, and the drink leak through the porous vessels, then they are happy, for the dead man's spirit has eaten and drunk all he wants. The widow, at the end of the year, has the bones of her deceased lord dug up and placed in bed with her. For one whole year she sleeps every night with the dead man's bones. Having suffered penance for two years she has the bones permanently placed at the entrance to her house, or over the door.

Another custom, almost as unique, is observed by a Central American tribe. The body is placed in a deep pit, large enough to seat all the wives, and such of the relatives as must die with the deceased. Around the dead body, in solemn silence, sit the living, while the friends are fasting, feasting, and dancing on top of the ground. This continues for two days, when, at the proper time, dozens of strong men surround the pit and proceed to fill it up—the living being buried alive with the dead. Trees are planted around the last resting place of the family. If a mother die in child-bed, and the child be living, the infant is buried alive on its mother's breast, to enable it to obtain food in the next world.

In India to-day, in this nineteenth century, the wife is buried alive with her deceased husband, and the new born children are cast into the rivers for the fish to eat.

The kings and nobles of the early races of the Pacific Coast were frequently cremated, as this gave the succeeding king or noble an opportunity of satisfying the thirst for blood, and also to get rid of any obnoxious individual who was in the way. The ashes were placed in urns made of silver and gold. This was deposited in the temple or palace, at the feet of their patron saint, and a statue of the dead placed over it. In Central America, the head of the deceased was cut off and boiled. The skull was then afterwards fitted up to resemble the individual in life, and used for the head of his statue.

Embalming was also practiced by some of the aborigines. Their process was the following: The dead body was suspended over a slow fire of herbs and green boughs. Here it would dry and smoke for many days, until all the moisture was abstracted, and only dry skin and bones remained. In this condition many mummified bodies were preserved in the temples, where they were suspended on the walls for centuries.

Embalming, although of ancient origin, was never practiced extensively in any country. In the islands of Fuerteventura it was used, but the process is now lost. The preserved body was surrounded with aromatic branches and tanned skins of the hog or goat, and placed in caves. The Peruvians of Incas, the Gouanches, and the Egyptians, at the time of the Pharaohs, were the only people who practiced mummification to any extent. The art is entirely lost. I examined several Egyptian

mummies, some of which were four thousand years old.
The skulls had been bared to inspect the bones of the
face. In these the embalming process seems to have
been the following: The bodies were wrapped in cloths
and then covered with a layer of pitch or tar, again a
layer of cloth and another covering of pitch, and this
continued until a thickness of one half to two inches
was obtained. The whole body was covered—perfectly
hermetically sealed from head to foot, and as indestruct-
ible and impervious as time itself. The bones looked
as fresh as though death occurred recently. The modern device of electro-plating dead bodies cannot be more
lasting than the Egyptian embalming of four thousand
or five thousand years ago.

Relative to the future state, the beliefs of the American aborigines very closely resemble the myths of older
countries, particularly those of the Orientals. For
example, the Apaches believe the wicked people to
inhabit rattlesnakes after death.

Sparks from a volcano are supposed to be villains
sent forth to torture the people.

"Will-o'-the-wisp" is a witch hunting for spirits.

The greatest superstition is attached to dreams by all
the aborigines. It is believed that while a person sleeps
some evil spirit takes possession of the body and actually accomplishes what the individual dreams.

A shadow is supposed to be the individual's other
self.

When portraits and photographs were first taken of
the tribes inhabiting the Gila Valley, the artists nar-
rowly escaped with their lives, as it was believed that
the "impression," or portrait, was the spirit transferred

by some magic power to the possessor of the photograph or picture.

As we have seen, the Aztecs were formed out of pieces of bone from the lower regions, so do they believe that wherever their bones are there also must be the spirit.

The souls of Sonoras dwell in caves.

The Tlascaltecs believe with the Hindoos that the souls of the dead return to earth and enter animals. The good souls enter clouds, precious gems, and birds of beautiful plumage; but the common and wicked souls pass into the inferior animals. Reincarnation was also believed in by several tribes. The Aztec souls are permitted to return to earth once a year to feast with their friends.

Note the similarity of our accepted myths of the old world.

The resurrection of the Egyptian Osiris, Orpheus, and Eurydice. Mithraic mysteries of Persia. The resurrection of the lifeless Sita in India. The Eleusinian mysteries permits the return of Kore to Demeter for one half of every year.

The metamorphoses in Celtic and Druidic mysteries in Gaul and Britain.

The Aztec confederacy, or ancient Mexicans, and before them the Iroquois and Toltecs, non-nomadic or towns-people, occupied northern Mexico, New Mexico, and Arizona, now represented by the Pueblos, Pimas, Moquis, Maricopas, and Pápagos. The prehistoric and early races, whose civilization and architectural progress have been the marvel of the world, building as they did large cities, houses, temples, and palaces of great splendor,* and aqueducts for the supply of water and irrigating purposes. They cultivated gardens and fields which supplied them with food to eat and clothes to wear. Their burial places were frequently within their own houses; also in caves, mounds, shafts, natural and artificial sarcophagi situated on their own premises or in adjoining caverns or cliffs.

The temple-pyramid in Mexico is a superstructure of royal graves. The remains were placed in a sarcophagus, one on top of the other, until the pyramid reaches nearly one hundred feet in height, by several hundred feet at its base.   *Walter W. Bradley.*

The ruins are justly called the "American Pompeii," and continue to attract merited attention from the scientific world. At the present writing, Professor Frank Cushing has charge of an exploring expedition in Arizona, under the direction of the Smithsonian Institute. Report reaches us that the ruins of a large city, "Los Muertos," he calls it, has been discovered and explored. This is situated on Salt River, near the junction of the Gila. As early as 1697, Father Keno made explorations in this same district, when he was establishing Jesuit Missions. He speaks of discovering extensive ruins, and a considerable population. Prior to this, the Spanish General, Coronado, in writing to the King of Spain, speaks of the ruins and of the people. Professor Cushing has discovered two thousand skeletons and mummified human remains; besides valuable prehistoric pottery, idols, utensils, and armaments of war and the chase, and for domestic purposes, etc., are exhumed.

---

* Using flakes of selenite for windows, and far ahead of Europeans at a similar period of civilization.

This will enrich the Smithsonian Institute, and the Bureau of Ethnology and Anthropology.

It is a source of regret that California does not take more interest in her prehistoric dwellers, and gather collections that would be invaluable to the scientific world. These could be collected at little expense, as many of them are at our very doors.

It is estimated that Los Muertos had a population of twenty-five thousand people, and that the "Seven Cities" along the Gila Valley represent the ruins of a population of more than two hundred thousand souls.

Wheat, barley, and corn, fabric, etc., indicate the high degree of civilization that these people enjoyed.

It is the opinion that some great calamity befell these people, like that of the inhabitants of Herculaneum and Pompeii, otherwise our ancient cities would probably be inhabited to-day. Earthquakes and volcanic eruptions have killed many of these people, and freighted more away, besides laying their flourishing cities in ruins. Several human bodies are found beneath walls as the excavation continues. The walls and temples are not mouldering away, but broken up and laid low on the ground. The people, except a mere remnant, have probably gone south, built the palaces and temples of the Mayas of Yucatan, and, indeed, the halls of the Incas of Peru.

The present bodies are certainly several hundred years old, and in all probability belong to the Aztec race.

One thing is certain, says *La Voce del Popolo*, that these remains belong to a race entirely different from the Indians who now inhabit the region where the mummies were found. The sealing of the cave, and the absence of the usual implements and utensils, may indicate that they were buried at the time of the conquest. The exact date of burial must, for the present, at least, remain a mystery.

From our best geological and archæological data the American aborigines are supposed to antedate our anthropophagous ancestors, from the wilds of Asia, by many thousands of years.

4

www.ingramcontent.com/pod-product-compliance
Lightning Source LLC
Chambersburg PA
CBHW031321280626
47169CB00019B/2603